It was then that a most **unusual** affair
unfurled while we chomped on our chocolate éclairs.

The zoo café staff were a funny old team.

A rhino was cooking.

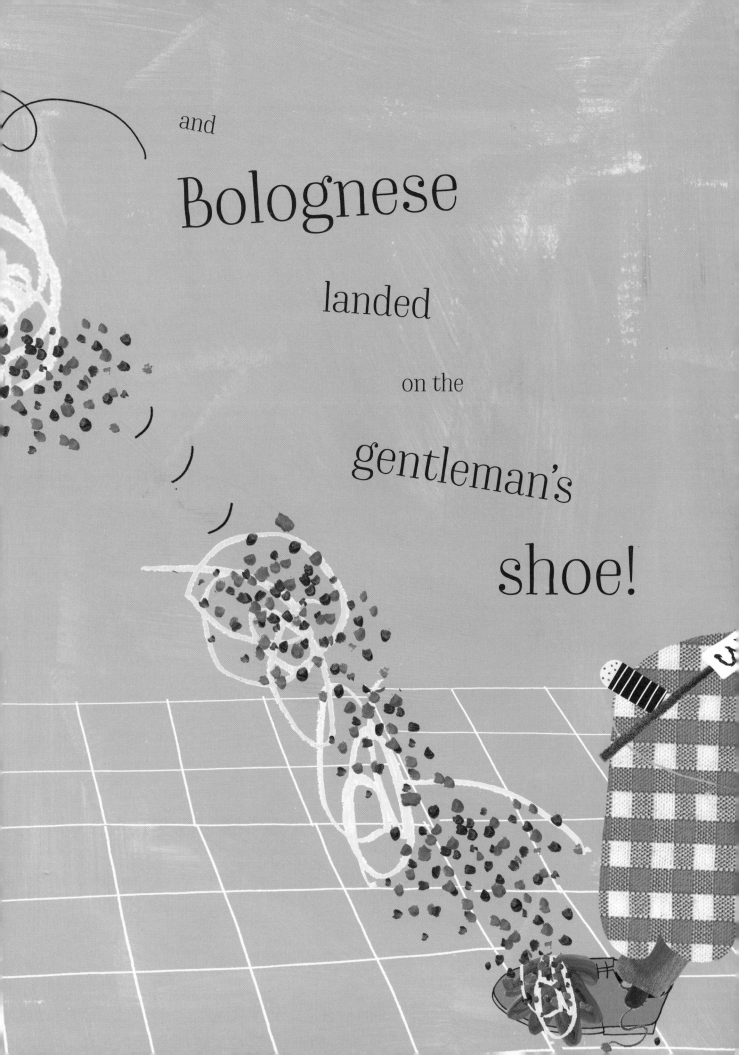

and

Bolognese

landed

on the

gentleman's

shoe!

An ice-cream sundae was next to go flying
at speed through the air where
people were dining.

An elegant lady,
dressed all in pink,
had just sat down
for some cake
and a drink.

Here came poor Mabel, delivering dessert
to a girl and her mum (in a nice flowery skirt).

She wobbled to the left . . .

She wobbled to the right . . .

She tried to keep steady with all of her might, BUT . . .

The strawberry sundae
was piled so **high**,
she struggled to hold it.
(She really did try.)
But she needed to dodge
a grumpy brown bear

HIC!

and off it shot into the **poor** lady's **hair!**

A really ravenous fellow named Tony,
(who was patiently awaiting his hot macaroni)
was soon to endure a much longer wait
when his cheesy lunch was the next ill-fated plate.

With the tasty meal held aloft on a tray,
Mabel approached and started to **sway**.

She wobbled to the left...

She wobbled to the right...

She tried to keep steady
with all of her might,

BUT...

Like a frisbee, the macaroni **zoomed** past the door, then

splattered
all
over
the
dining-room
floor.

Mabel felt glum splashing
people with food.
It really did put her
in a very sad mood.

She swept up the mess then perched on a stool.
Oh dear! Mabel felt like a bit of a fool.
Everyone knew that it wasn't her fault.
The hiccups were making her jitter and jolt.

Her friends wanted to help. They felt really bad.
They didn't like Mabel looking so sad.
"I've got it!" said Tony. "Let's make it our mission
to distract her quick smart from this frightful condition."

"We could blast her with music,

or pirouette on ice-skates.

"Teach her aerobics and stretching with weights."

"She could fly way up high,
walk the wings of a plane,

loop the loop in the sky,
then fly back again."

"We could put something
squirmy into her pocket!"

"Or catapult her to the moon in a rocket!"

Just then Bob thought of a **better** idea,
and whispered, "Come closer so you can all hear.
We'll all work together. We'll give her a **fright**.
The hiccups will flee and she'll soon be all right."

"You go over there. Hide beside Bert the boar.
We'll crouch down behind this very big door.

When Mabel comes out with her next cake or drink,
we'll be ready and jump out before she can blink."

Mabel was focused and trying hard **not** to shake,

as she nervously headed over to serve Sid the snake.

Her friends waited ... Then sprung and, without further ado,

cured Mabel's hiccups with a very loud

BOO!

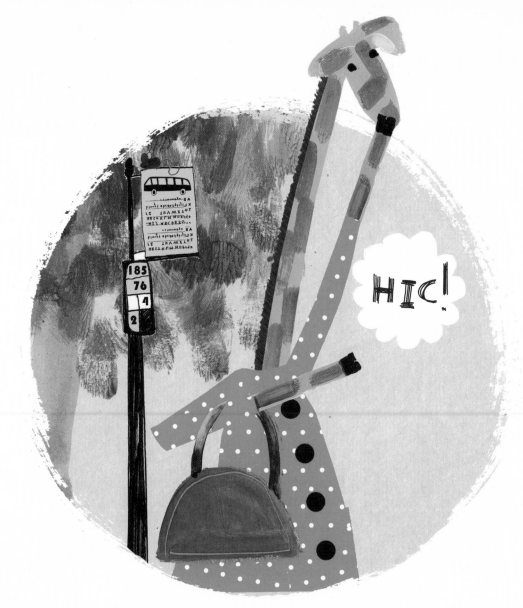

To Anna, Hayden, Henry and Mabel x

And a very special thanks to Ada, the super narrator x

ENORMOUS thanks to Holly, Sally and the Tate team
for making this book possible

First published 2018 by order of the Tate Trustees
by Tate Publishing, a division of Tate Enterprises Ltd,
Millbank, London SW1P 4RG

www.tate.org.uk/publishing
Text and artwork © Lisa Levis
First published 2018

ISBN 978 1 84976 592 3

Distributed in the United States and Canada by ABRAMS, New York
Library of Congress Control Number applied for
Printed in China by Toppan Leefung Printing Ltd
Colour reproduction by DL Imaging Ltd, London